Diego Saves a Butterfly

adapted by Lara Bergen
based on the original teleplay by Madellaine Paxson
illustrated by Warner McGee

Ready-to-Read

SIMON SPOTLIGHT/NICK JR.
New York   London   Toronto   Sydney

visit us at www.abdopublishing.com

Reinforced library bound edition published in 2009 by Spotlight, a division of ABDO Publishing Group, 8000 West 78th Street, Edina, Minnesota 55439. Published by agreement with Simon Spotlight, an imprint of Simon & Schuster Children's Publishing Division.

SIMON SPOTLIGHT

An imprint of Simon & Schuster Children's Publishing Division
1230 Avenue of the Americas, New York, NY 10020
Copyright © 2007 Viacom International Inc. Based on the TV series *Go, Diego, Go!*™ as seen on Nick Jr.® NICK JR., *Go, Diego, Go!*, and all related titles, logos, and characters are trademarks of Viacom International Inc.
All rights reserved, including the right of reproduction in whole or in part in any form.
SIMON SPOTLIGHT, READY-TO-READ, and colophon are registered trademarks of Simon & Schuster.

Library of Congress Cataloging-in-Publication Data

This title was previously cataloged with the following information:

Bergen, Lara.
  Diego saves a butterfly / adapted by Lara Bergen ; illustrated by Warner McGee.
    p. cm. -- (Ready-to-read. Level 1; #3)
  "Based on the TV series Go, Diego, Go! as seen on Nick Jr."
  I. McGee, Warner, ill. II. Go, Diego, Go! (Television program). III. Title. IV. Series.
PZ7.B44985 Die 2007
[E]--dc22   2006020321

ISBN-13: 978-1-59961-435-9 (reinforced library bound edition)
ISBN-10: 1-59961-435-9 (reinforced library bound edition)

All Spotlight books have reinforced library binding
and are manufactured in the United States of America.

Hi! I am .
DIEGO

Look at this  !
COCOON

Do you know what is inside?

It is a  !
BUTTERFLY

It is a Blue Morpho !
BUTTERFLY

"Let me see!" says .

BABY JAGUAR

Oh, no!

The  flew away.

BUTTERFLY

I think

BABY JAGUAR

scared the .

BUTTERFLY

Do not worry, .

BABY JAGUAR

 can help us

CLICK

find the .

BUTTERFLY

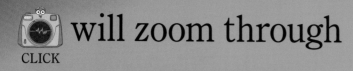 will zoom through

the rainforest to look for

the .

Is this the ?
BUTTERFLY

No, this is a .
LADYBUG

Is this the ?
BUTTERFLY

Yes!

BUTTERFLIES live
in the rainforest.
But this **BUTTERFLY**
is in a **CAVE**.
The **CAVE** is cold!

We have to bring the  BUTTERFLY
back to the warm rainforest.
Come on!

Now we are in the .
CAVE

But the  is so dark!
CAVE

 can help us see.
RESCUE PACK

Here is !

Can help us see?

No.

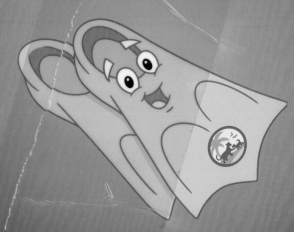

Can a help us see?

Yes!

There is the  !

BUTTERFLY

"I am too cold to fly," says the 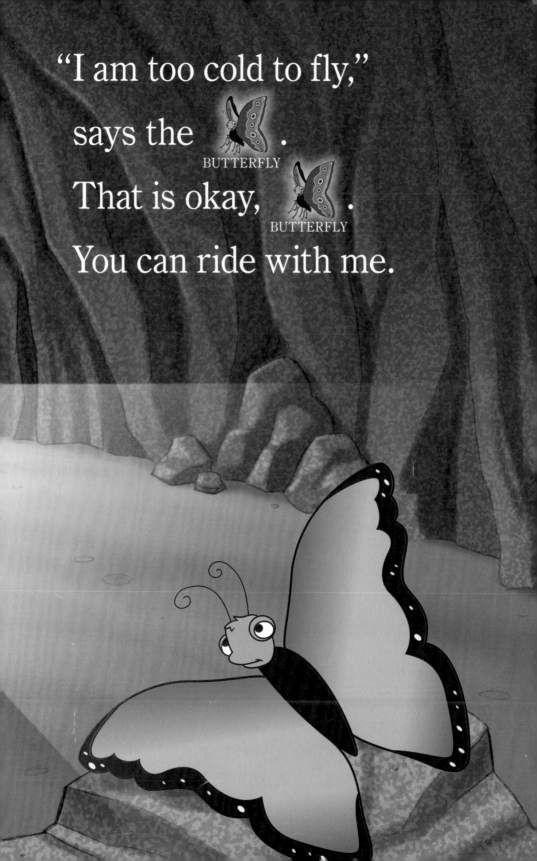 BUTTERFLY.
That is okay, BUTTERFLY.
You can ride with me.

BUTTERFLIES like to sip juice

from FRUIT .

Do you see any  ?

FRUIT

"Yum!" says the .
BUTTERFLY

The was good.
FRUIT

The is warm
BUTTERFLY

again.

Now she can fly!

To the rainforest!

Come on!

Oh, no!
There is a big  !
BIRD
The  is afraid of  .
BUTTERFLY   BIRDS

When the  opens its
wings, the flies away.
The BUTTERFLY is brave!

BUTTERFLY

BIRD

BUTTERFLY

We made it back to the rainforest. But where is  ?

BABY JAGUAR

"Here I am," says  .

BABY JAGUAR

"I do not want to scare the .

BUTTERFLY

I want to be friends."

"Me too!" says the .

BUTTERFLY

Thanks for helping us save the !

BUTTERFLY

And thanks for helping

BABY JAGUAR

make a new friend too!